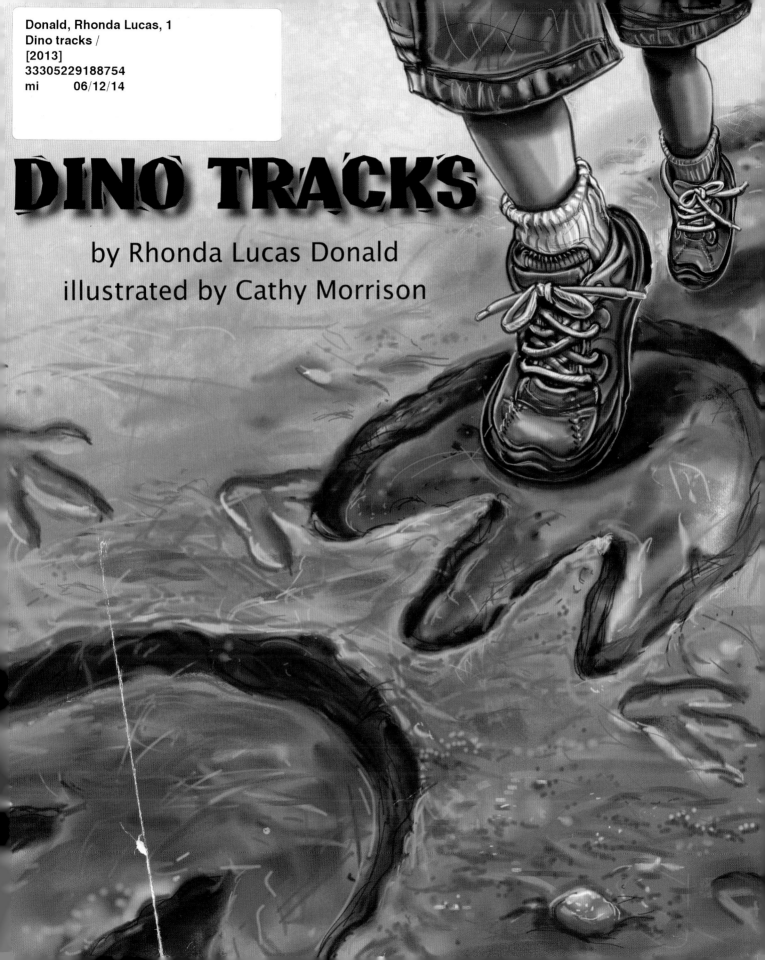

DINO TRACKS

by Rhonda Lucas Donald

illustrated by Cathy Morrison

Down by the river and in the rock—
what are these marks I see?
In some you can lie and curl up inside,
and some have toes of three.

Down by the river of long ago,
dinosaurs once roamed.
Although they are gone, their footprints walk on—
forever set in stone.

T'was quite long ago in Hadley, Mass.,
a farm boy plowed a field.
What he turned up, created a fuss—
what had his work revealed?

Across the vast surface of stone so hard,
huge three-toed prints abound.
They looked like a bird, but the size—*my word!*
Fossil dino tracks he'd found!

Look at the footprints the creatures made.
What do the marks help prove?
The shape of the feet help show what it might eat;
the spacing, how it moved.

Tracks by themselves show a lone dino,
but many may form a herd.
The marks left behind by tails is a find—
tail dragging was not preferred!

Out on the meadow found in the West,
two sets of tracks we spot.
One measures higher than a small tire,
the other's a few-inch dot.

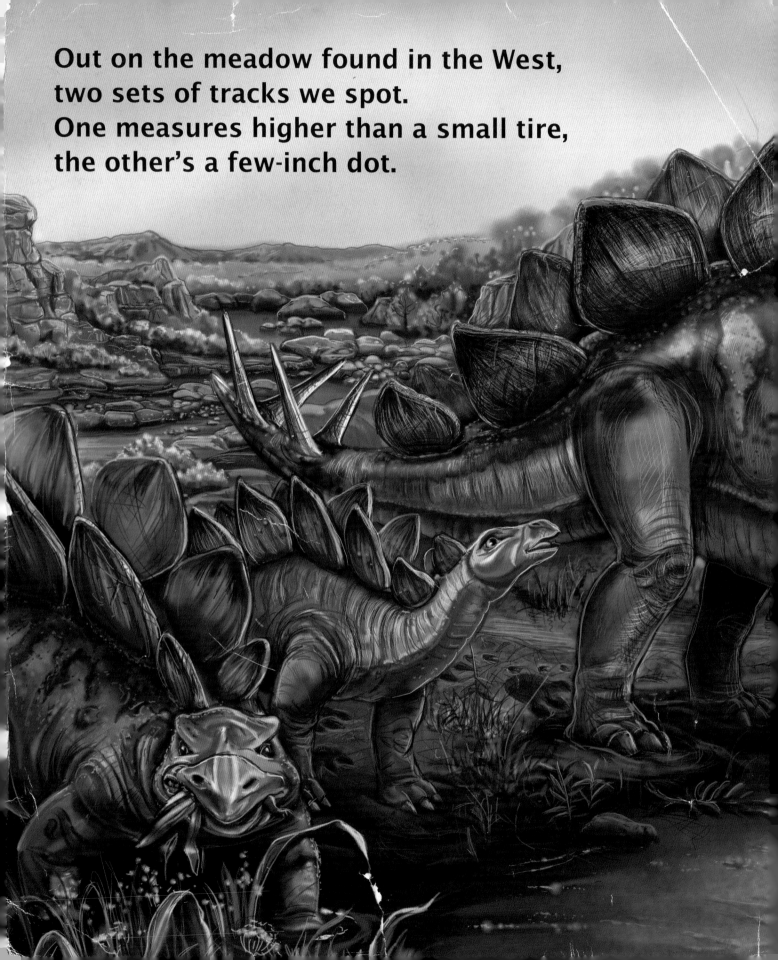

Down by the river where crocs were thick,
are tracks of dainty feet.
They skitter on by—it's best to be sly—
or hungry crocs they'd meet.

Down by the river so long ago,
the dinosaurs had arrived.
Though crocs rule the day, they'd better make way,
for dinos are bound to thrive.

Over the sands of a strip of beach,
huge reptiles flew so high.
This spot in the sand is where they would land,
their track marks cannot lie.

Down to the sand in a gliding bump,
the giants touched the shore.
They gave a short hop, and came to a stop,
and walked off on all fours.

Dinosaurs lived at a time when Earth
was a warm and steamy place.
But even so, the poles were still cold,
and there we find a trace.

Treading the lands of the southern pole,
the hunters left their sign.
Although it seems strange, some dinos did range
in this chilly polar clime.

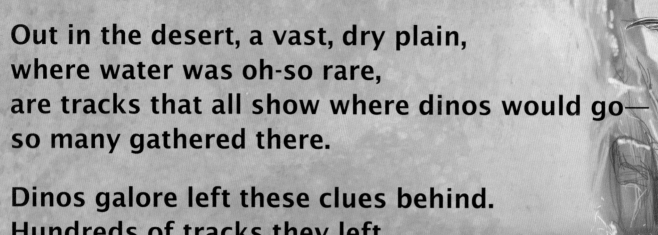

Out in the desert, a vast, dry plain,
where water was oh-so rare,
are tracks that all show where dinos would go—
so many gathered there.

Dinos galore left these clues behind.
Hundreds of tracks they left.
What was the cause that made them all pause?
A watering hole, I'll bet.

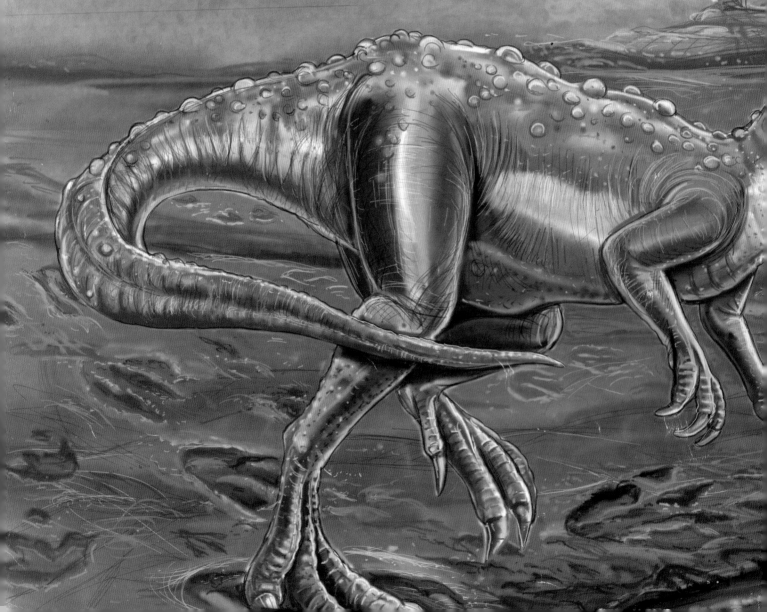

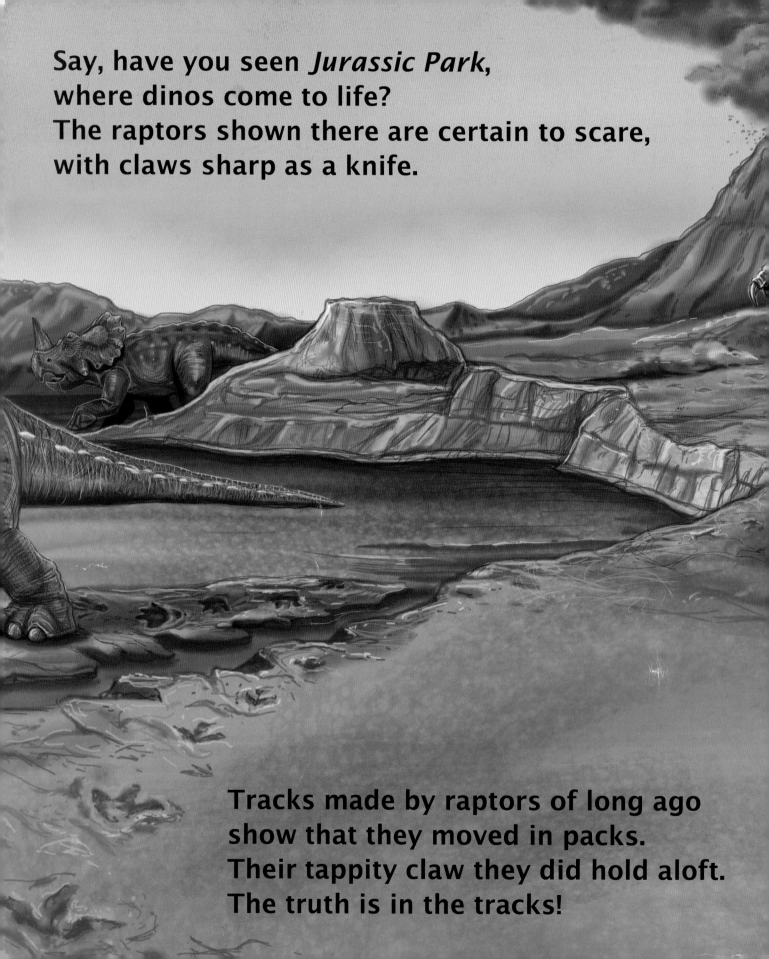

Say, have you seen *Jurassic Park*,
where dinos come to life?
The raptors shown there are certain to scare,
with claws sharp as a knife.

Tracks made by raptors of long ago
show that they moved in packs.
Their tappity claw they did hold aloft.
The truth is in the tracks!

Out of a river and up a bank,
the dinosaurs had to climb.
They clambered ashore, on two feet or four,
and left their prints behind.

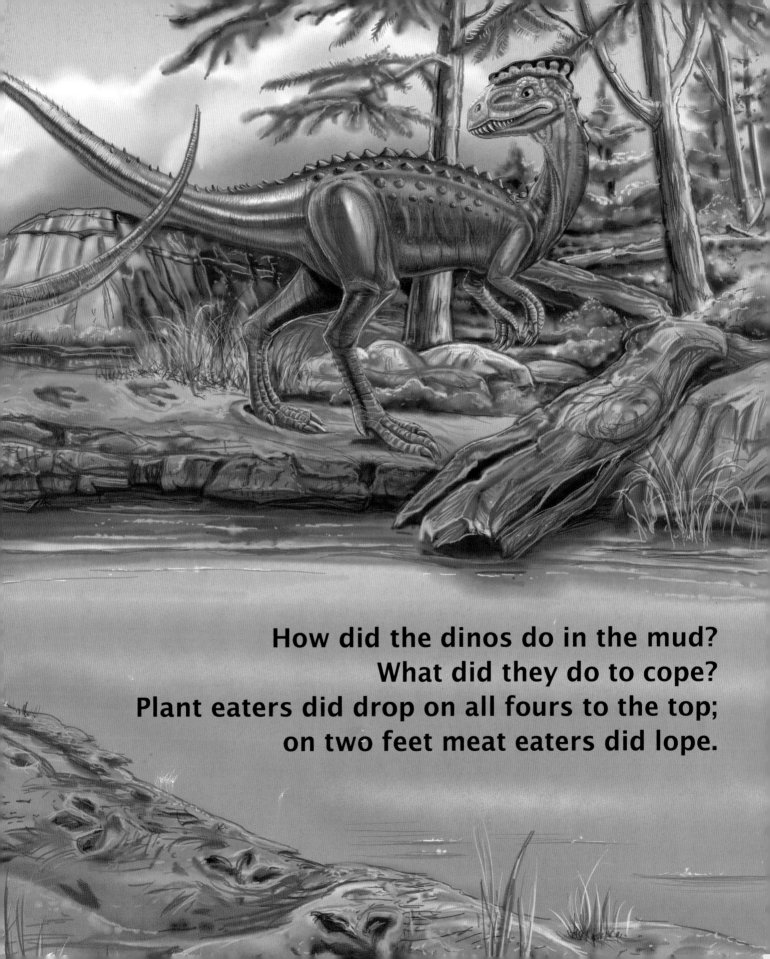

How did the dinos do in the mud?
What did they do to cope?
Plant eaters did drop on all fours to the top;
on two feet meat eaters did lope.

Inside a bank by an ancient shore,
a dinosaur dug a den.
Tucked deep down inside, two youngsters did hide
with an adult that squeezed in.

Down in a burrow, safe from the world,
digging dinosaurs were snug.
To escape from the heat or hunters of meat—
that's why they must have dug.

Step back in time to a long-lost land,
where dinos ruled the Earth.
Although they are gone, their traces live on,
and they are of great worth.

Much from the traces and tracks we learn;
they have so much to say.
Clues in the rocks show they swam and flocked.
Can you read the tracks today?

For Creative Minds

Dinosaur Puzzles and Scientists

How do we really know that dinosaurs once roamed this earth? What did they look like? What kinds of dinosaurs were there and how many different kinds? When did they live? What did they eat—meat, plants, or both? How did they move? In what types of habitats did they live? How big or little were they? What kind of skin did they have? Did they care for and teach their young like humans do? Or did the young survive on instinct as many animals do today? These are all dinosaur puzzles.

Can you imagine trying to put a puzzle together without knowing what the picture looks like? That's what scientists do when putting together bits of pieces of information about dinosaurs. Many different types of scientists use clues to learn about dinosaurs. They dig to find and study dinosaur remains and tracks. They are learning new things all the time. Sometimes new information is uncovered that causes scientists to reconsider things they had previously thought had been correct. Scientists don't always agree with one another'sideas. For example, some scientists might not agree with other scientists' explanations of the trackways in this book. Questioning one another helps scientists to learn and piece together pictures of these ancient animals and their behavior.

Paleontologists study the fossils of plants and animals. They find bits and pieces of skeletons (body fossils) that they put together—even if they don't have all the pieces.

Ichnologists study the behavior of living things based on things left behind: footprints, nests, eggs, and even poop.

Paleoichnologists study fossilized footprints, nests, eggs, and even fossilized poop (trace fossils).

Geologists study rock layers. They can tell when a dinosaur lived and what the environment was like at the time.

Biologists help "flesh out" the bones to understand what dinosaurs might have looked like and how they may have moved and behaved.

Chemists study fossilized skin and feathers to help us know what colors dinosaurs might have been.

Artists use all this information to make paintings and sculptures that bring the ancient creatures to life.

Maybe you'll be a dinosaur scientist when you grow up!

Dinosaurs: True or False

Are the following statements true or false?

1. The word dinosaur means "fearfully great lizard." But dinosaurs weren't lizards at all. They were a different kind of reptile.

2. All dinosaurs walked upright on two feet.

3. Dinosaurs only had scaly skin.

4. The largest dinosaurs were longer than four school buses and nearly as tall as a four-story building.

5. Some dinosaurs were about the size of chickens.

6. Like animals today, dinosaurs lived all over the world in all kinds of habitats from swamps to the cold poles.

7. Some dinosaurs were meat eaters (carnivores). Many others were plant eaters (herbivores). And others ate both meat and plants (omnivores).

8. The earliest known dinosaur lived about 250 million years ago. Most of the dinosaurs vanished 65 million years ago.

9. Today's birds descended from dinosaurs.

10. A single footprint or handprint is called a track. Many tracks together make a trackway. The dinosaur tracks and trackways that we see today have been turned into rocks or fossilized.

Answers: 1) True. 2) False. Some walked upright on straight legs. Some walked on all fours the way dogs and cats do. And some walked on just their hind legs like an ostrich. 3) False: Some dinosaurs had scaly skin and others had feathers! 4) True. 5) True. 6) True. 7) True. 8) True—Scientists think that the impact of a giant asteroid may have done them in. Climate change and volcano eruptions may also have been to blame. 9) True. 10) True—Millions of years ago, a dinosaur walked across a patch of soft ground. Its feet left impressions in the ground just as you do when you walk on a beach. If the footprints weren't washed away or trampled over, they would dry in the sun and harden. Next, a layer of mud, sand, or other sediment filled in the prints. Over many years, more sediment built up on top of the track layer. The weight and pressure from so many layers caused the mud around the tracks to turn to rock. Fossils were born!

Dinosaur Tracks

Many trackways are found along ancient streams, lakes, or beaches. They may contain the tracks of one animal or hundreds. Tracks can tell us about the animal that made them. They can tell us whether the animal was walking, running, resting, or slipping in the mud. They can tell us if an animal traveled alone or in a herd. They can even tell us what the animal ate!

There are three main dinosaur groups that left tracks.

- Theropods had sharp teeth, walked on two back feet, and had short front legs and feet. These meat eaters left narrow, three-toed tracks with signs of sharp claws.
- Sauropods had long necks, walked on all four feet, and were plant-eaters. They left two pairs of rounded tracks. The back feet were often much larger than the front feet, so the tracks are different sizes.
- Ornithopods walked on two bird-like feet and were plant eaters. They left three-toed, rounded tracks.

Identifying the tracks by dinosaur group is easy. It's like telling a cat's footprint from a dog's footprint. Knowing exactly which species made the track is hard. If scientists find a skeleton nearby and the foot bones match the tracks, they can make a match.

Can you identify to which dinosaur group these tracks belong?

Look through the book to identify any of the tracks in the art. By looking at the tracks, can you tell if the dinosaurs were meat-eaters or plant-eaters?

Were there many types of dinosaurs leaving tracks or just one? If you were a scientist, what could you infer from that observation?

How big is your footprint compared to a dinosaur track?

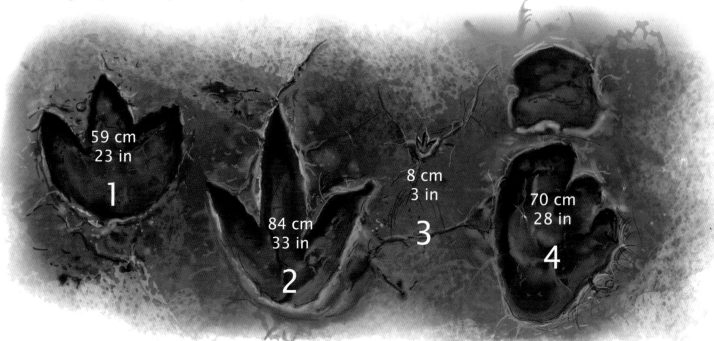

59 cm
23 in
1

84 cm
33 in
2

8 cm
3 in
3

70 cm
28 in
4

Answers: 1) Ornithopods. 2) Theropods. 3) Theropods. 4) Sauropods.

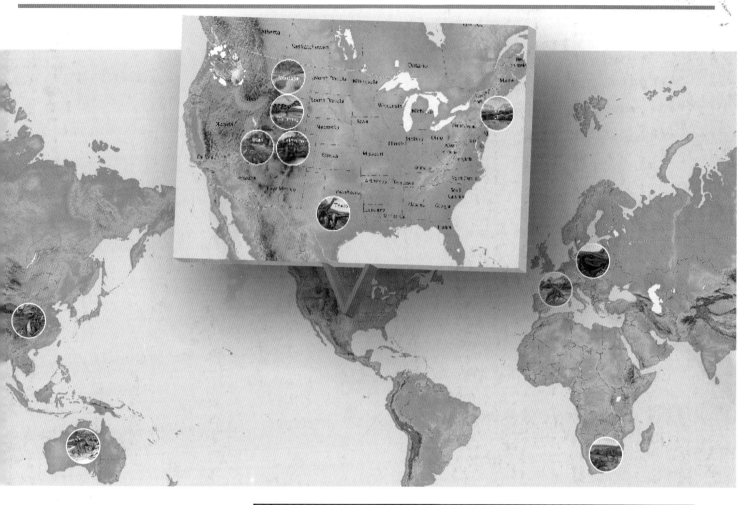

Dinosaurs lived just about everywhere. Look at the map to see where tracks mentioned in this book were found. Are there any tracks near where you live?

Scientists have estimated how many million years ago the tracks were made.

Location	Million Years Ago
Glen Rose, Texas, USA	110
Hadley, Massachusetts, USA	225–220
Morrison, Colorado, USA	150
Holy Cross Mountains, Poland	250
Crayssac, France	150
Victoria, Australia	115–100
Zion National Park, Utah, USA	190
Shandong Province, China	120
Lesotho, Africa	200
Lima, Montana, USA	95
Hell Creek Formation, Wyoming, USA	67

To my little dino trackers: Nev, Richard, Roy, Charlotte, and Molly.—RLD

For my grandson, Konnor Brown, and all the future paleoichnologists out there. And a big "thank you!" to Matthew Mossbrucker and the entire staff of the Morrison Natural History Museum in Morrison, Colorado for allowing us back in the fossil lab for a sneak peek of the excavation of the partial skull of "Kevin," the Apatosaurus.—CM

Thanks to Jeffrey A. Wilson, Associate Professor, Department of Earth & Environmental Sciences and Associate Curator, Museum of Paleontology at the University of Michigan, for verifying the information in this book.

Library of Congress Cataloging-in-Publication Data

Donald, Rhonda Lucas, 1962-
  Dino tracks / by Rhonda Lucas Donald ; illustrated by Cathy Morrison.
    pages cm
  Audience: 4-8.
  Audience: K to grade 3.
  ISBN 978-1-60718-619-9 (English hardcover) -- ISBN 978-1-60718-631-1 (English pbk.) -- ISBN 978-1-60718-643-4 (English ebook (downloadable)) -- ISBN 978-1-60718-667-0 (interactive English/Spanish ebook (web-based)) -- ISBN 978-1-60718-655-7 (Spanish ebook (downloadable))
  1. Paleontology--Juvenile literature. 2. Dinosaurs--Juvenile literature. I. Morrison, Cathy, illustrator. II. Title.
  QE714.5.D66 2013
  567.9--dc23
                                2012045093

Las dino-huellas: Translated into Spanish by Rosalyna Toth
Lexile® Level: 700
Key phrases for educators: dinosaurs, fossils, scientists/jobs, maps, rhyme & rhythm

Manufactured in China, June, 2013
This product conforms to CPSIA 2008
First Printing

Sylvan Dell Publishing
Mt. Pleasant, SC 29464
www.SylvanDellPublishing.com